STITCH HEAD

THE SPIDER'S LAIR

To Stephanie Thwaites —
agent, corner fighter,
occasional therapist
~Guy Bass

For Frankiecarlo and Dante,
to read in your house by the lake.
~Pete Williamson

Stitch Head

THE SPIDER'S LAIR

GUY BASS

ILLUSTRATED BY
PETE WILLIAMSON

capstone
young readers

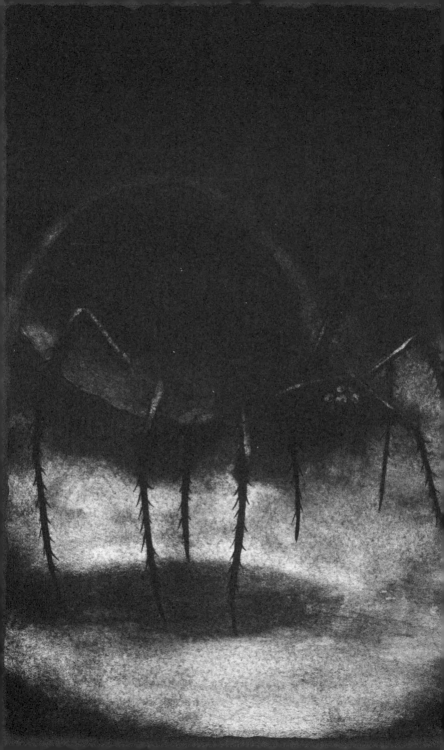

ODE TO THE
SPIDER

How do I love thee? Let me count the ways.
I love thee for thy venom
And thy stony-hearted gaze.

How do I love thee? Let me count thine eyes.
All eight of them, to match your legs
That no one can disguise.

How do I love thee? Let me count thy fangs.
Oh dear! It seems I'm bitten,
You must have hunger pangs.

How do I love thee? Let me end my rhyme,
Your venom's started working
And I'm running out of time.

How do I love thee? Let me drift away …
To dream again of spiders,
'Tis a fitting final day!

WELCOME TO
GRUBBERS NUBBIN
(POPULATION 612)

YE OLDEN DAYS
(SOMETIME BEFORE
YESTERYEAR)

DEAD OF NIGHT
(Madder than a dog with ten legs)

MAD MUSING No. 13

"No visitors!"

From *The Occasionally Scientific Writings of Professor Erasmus Erasmus*

"Gadsbodkins! Look out!"

The carriage rolled quickly through the rain-beaten street, the horse's breath puffing out in rhythmic clouds as the whip struck its flank. Atop the carriage, an old man cried out as the townsfolk scattered in terror.

"Sorry! Beg your pardon! Please, out of the way! My most sincere apologies! Coming through!" he shouted as the carriage plowed through the town.

An old lady cradling a baby leaped out of the way into a deep puddle on the side of the road. "Dirty rotten goat! You nearly squished my granddaughter!" she bellowed. She checked on the baby and plucked a soaking doll out of the puddle.

"A thousand pardons, madam!" called the old man as the carriage sped out of town.

"Shove it up yer nostrils!" cried the old

woman, angrily shaking her fist. She shook her head and handed the baby its doll. "See, Arabella? That's the problem with folk these days — they ain't got no respect. Which is why you should always kick first, ask questions later."

"Kick!" squeaked the baby.

"Awww, your first word," cooed the old lady.

The carriage made its way up the hill through the driving rain. The old man peered into the darkness. Ahead loomed a dark, forbidding shape — *the castle.*

"There it is!" the old man cried. "We made it!"

He jumped down from the carriage and hurried to the castle's Great Door. He hammered on it with both hands, crying, "Erasmus! Erasmus! It is I! Open this door, I beg of you! In fact, I politely insist!"

The pause that followed was longer than you would have expected from even the most unwelcoming of castles. Then, at last, a cry rang out from inside.

"No visitors!"

"Please be so kind as to let me in! It is I!" the old man replied.

"I?" said the voice.

"*Me!*"

"Me?"

"Not *you*, me!"

"You? You *who*?"

"Yoo hoo to you, too! Gadsbodkins, it is *Edmund*! Let me in!" the man insisted.

The silence that followed was finally broken by the voice behind the door. "What do *you* want?"

"I am in desperate need of your help!" cried Edmund. "Now, please kindly open this door or by my frozen underwear, I shall be forced to knock again!"

"Help? I don't help!" hissed the voice, as if trying to divine the meaning of the word. "I'm a mad professor! There's nothing mad about helping!"

"What I ask of you is most assuredly mad! Madder than mad! Madder than a dog with ten legs!" insisted the old man. "Now I beg you, in the name of all that is good and holy, please open this door!"

Another pause followed. The old man continued to stand shivering in the rain. Finally, he heard the *CLUNK* and *KRONG* of the Great Door. It swung open. A spindly lizard of a man in a white coat took a single step into the moonlight, wringing his hands madly.

"I actually *made* a ten-legged dog last week," he said with a sneer. "Now what do you want? Out with it! I am at a crucial point in my mad experiment — you have ten seconds before I close this door in your face. AhaHA!"

"I need only five," replied the old man, disappearing behind his carriage. He re-emerged moments later, stumbling back through the rain, struggling to carry something in both arms. It was wrapped in a blanket and was almost as large as the old man himself.

"What do you have there?" demanded

Professor Erasmus. The old man held out his arms. It took the professor a moment to realize he was carrying a dead body.

"I wish for the impossible," replied the old man. "I wish for you to bring the dead back to life."

The professor's eyes grew wide. The old man shivered silently in the rain. Finally, a jagged, maniacal grin spread across the professor's face.

"Well, why didn't you say so before? Come on in . . . AhahaHA! AhaaHAAA!"

TEN YEARS LATER

KING OF THE CASTLE

(Look out below)

**Blood Succor
Anti-vampire Tonic**

For the treatment of chronic or
persistent bloodlust.
Two spoonfuls nightly until
cravings subside.

(Warning: may cause loss of fangs)

Stitch Head made his way through the ruined, blackened corridors of Castle Grotteskew. A bitter wind whistled through the windows and snow gently fell through holes in the ceiling. Stitch Head wrapped his tiny, mismatched arms around himself to keep warm.

"Stitch Head . . ."

All at once, a dozen hideous, unnatural creatures emerged from the shadows, each more impossibly freakish than the last. Before long, Stitch Head found himself surrounded by a terrifying assortment of monstrosities. A slithering serpent with a human head. A giant eyeball with tentacle feet. A part-dog, part-cat, part-bat. A steam-powered skull. It was the stuff of *nightmares.*

"Stitch Head!" cried the skull, standing in Stitch Head's path. "A thousand thanks for that extra dose of Lunacy Lotion. It worked miracles. Now I feel one hundred percent less crazy!"

"No problem, Godfrey," said Stitch Head.

"Stitch Head! That Blood Succor tonic completely cured my vampirism!" said the dog-cat-bat. "I owe you one!"

"You're welcome, Bertram," replied Stitch Head.

"Your Savagery Salve worked like magic, Stitch Head," hissed the man-serpent. "I can't even remember the last time I attacked someone!"

"Glad I could help, Quentin," Stitch Head said.

Through corridor after corridor, Stitch Head found himself confronted by grateful creations.

"Thank you *so* much for the eye drops. I can finally see where I'm squirming!"

"Thanks for finding my phantom limb.

I knew I had left it lying around here somewhere . . ."

"Great work unblocking my toilet!"

Indeed, despite the creations' near-impossible monstrousness and stomach-wrenching ugliness, each one was more friendly than the last. Stitch Head simply nodded humbly and kept moving through the castle.

At last he arrived at the charred remains of a thick door barely hanging from its hinges. He pushed it open and stepped into the fire-blackened shadow of a once great hall. Inside, a dozen or so creations were busily carrying out repairs. In one corner, a massive, multitentacled octo-monster patched up holes in the wall. In another, a colossal lizard-beast chewed up and swallowed mounds of rubble in its great jaws.

"Uh, excuse me," said Stitch Head as a

wheel-footed wolf-woman zoomed past him at top speed. "Have you seen the Cr—"

"Look out BELOW!"

Stitch Head looked up to see a huge chunk of wood tumbling toward him. He leaped out of the way as the timber *CRRASSH!*-ed to the floor inches from where he'd been standing.

"Not AGAIN! Did I SQUASH anyone THIS time?" said a familiar voice. Stitch Head got to his feet and looked up. His best friend, the Creature, clung precariously to a scorched timber frame — all that was left of the roof.

"STITCH Head!" yelled the Creature, clambering down from the ceiling. The Creature was one of Professor Erasmus's most impressive creations — a huge, hulking monstrosity with a breathtakingly terrifying mix of unpleasant elements, including a tail and a spare arm.

"So what do you THINK?" it asked. "Pretty IMPRESSIVE work, huh? The EAST WING will be back to its GRIM, DEPRESSING self in NO time."

"You're doing a fantastic job, Creature," replied Stitch Head with a small smile. "Near-death experiences aside, that is . . ."

"I KNOW! I think I've found my CALLING. I LOVE being a BUILDING FOREMAN! All the pressure, all the responsibility, plus the YELLING . . ."

The Creature began striding around the room, shouting things like, "YOU there! More FLICKER in the lamp! More CREAK in that DOOR!"

"Actually, I don't think you have to yell," began Stitch Head.

"It's GREAT! I'm TELLING you, Stitch Head, you should BURN down the castle more OFTEN."

"It was an accident," said Stitch Head. He sighed, blushing a slightly darker shade of ash-gray than normal. "Actually, it'd be nice if everyone stopped talking about —"

"No one holds it AGAINST you. It's not EVERY day you get POSSESSED by an evil GHOST and try to DESTROY everything," boomed the Creature. "Anyway, the CREATIONS are all DELIGHTED to FINALLY have something to DO around here! Between that and all the HELP you're DISHING out, you COULDN'T be more

POPULAR! It's like you're KING of THE CASTLE!"

"I don't know about that," said Stitch Head, blushing again. It still felt strange to be out of the shadows. He had spent most of his almost-life locked away in a small room in the castle. Part of him missed that peace and quiet.

"At THIS rate," continued the Creature, leaning down to Stitch Head and whispering in his ear, "you MIGHT even get a CELEBRITY VIP INVITE to the castle Christmas PARTY!"

"Wait, aren't *you* organizing the castle Christmas party?" asked Stitch Head.

"YEP! It's going to be GREAT! Haven't gotten MY invitation yet, though . . . fingers CROSSED!"

"Do *I* get an invite?" said a voice.

Stitch Head and the Creature turned to see Arabella leaning against one of the many statues of Professor Erasmus that littered the castle. Arabella Guff was a girl from Grubbers Nubbin. She was fierce, fearless, and the only human Stitch Head had ever met (except for Professor Erasmus) who wasn't terrified of the castle and its inhabitants.

"ARABELLA!" the Creature cried. "We haven't seen you in so LONG! Where have you BEEN? We've MISSED you!"

"I've been busy," replied Arabella. She ruffled her already untidy and tangled hair and rubbed one of her boots on the back of her leg. Her pet monkey-bat, Pox (half-monkey, half-bat, entirely savage) fluttered down excitedly onto her shoulder and started hungrily gnawing on the tip of her left ear.

"So, what's new, Stitch Head?" Arabella said. "Burned down any castles lately?"

"It was an accident," said Stitch Head tiredly. "Anyway," he continued, eager to change the subject, "how's your grandma, Arabella? Is — is she any better?"

"That's the thing . . ." said Arabella. She tugged at her black dress, and then kicked the professor's statue. "Grandma went and *died* on me."

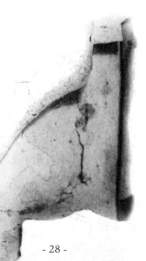

THE SECOND CHAPTER

ORPHANED
(Nowhere to go)

CAUTION:
CREATIONS AT WORK

DANGER OF FALLING STUFF
TAILS AND TRAILING TENTACLES MUST
BE WORN UP AT ALL TIMES

"Your grandmother . . . died?" said Stitch Head.

"Oh, ARABELLA!" the Creature cried. It stomped over to Arabella, picked her up in all three of its arms, and gave her an enormous hug.

"Hey! No cuddles! Don't make me kick your nose off," Arabella growled. The Creature nervously placed her back on the floor. "Anyways, dying's just one of them things . . . except maybe for you guys. See, Grandma was *really* old and sickly. And she *did* get a bit annoying toward the end, with all that ranting and raving. I don't even think she knew her own name, let alone mine. Then there was the *smell* . . . how come old people always smell like cabbage and dead flowers?"

"Well, uh, I'm sure she's gone to a better place," said Stitch Head.

"Definitely," nodded Arabella. "The

graveyard's almost as scary as Castle Grotteskew. I *love* it there."

"That's not exactly what I — never mind," said Stitch Head. A moment later, Arabella kicked the professor's statue so hard it tumbled to the ground with a *CRACK!*

"Uh, are you sure you're going to be okay?" asked Stitch Head gently.

Arabella scuffed the ground with the heel of her boot. "It's just, without Grandma, I'm all by myself. I ain't got nobody to look after me . . . not that I need any looking after!"

"Of course not," replied Stitch Head, hoping Arabella wouldn't kick anything else.

"But since I've got no family left, it's the orphanage for me," Arabella continued. "They're coming for me tomorrow. I'm here to say goodbye."

"What's an AWFULAGE?" the Creature asked. "It sounds AWFUL."

"An *orphanage* is where children go when they don't have anywhere else to go," said Stitch Head quietly.

"A prison for children — *that's* what an orphanage really is. They work you like dogs and feed you nothing but dried worms," said Arabella.

She put on a tough face and crossed her arms. "Still, it ain't nothing I can't handle."

"Arabella, I'm sorry . . ." began Stitch Head. Arabella was the bravest creature he'd ever met — creation or otherwise — but losing her family, home, and friends all at once? It was too much to bear.

"CAN'T someone from GRUBBERS NUBBIN look AFTER you?" cried the Creature.

"Yeah, right," Arabella said with a snort. "They'll be glad to see me go, on account of all the shouting and kicking I do."

Stitch Head scratched the back of his head and took a long, deep breath.

"But . . . but what if you're not there when they come for you?" he asked. "What if you just disappeared in the middle of the night, never to be seen again? How would the orphanage know where to find you?"

"What do you mean?" Arabella asked.

"I mean, you could come and live with us," Stitch Head replied. "Here, in the castle."

"What? With all the monsters and creatures and crazy things?" said Arabella. Her face suddenly lit up and a wide smile spread across her face. "You mean it?"

"Of course!" replied Stitch Head. "We can be your family."

"I . . . I dunno what to say," said Arabella, quickly wiping a tear from her eye.

"Say YES!" boomed the Creature. "Plus, you ARE kind of a HANDFUL — we'd be doing the AWFULAGE a FAVOR, taking you OFF their HANDS."

"Shut your nostrils, boil-brain! Or I'll kick you in the tail!" she barked.

"It's settled, then!" said Stitch Head. "When can you move in?"

"Ain't no time like the present! I'll just need to get a few things from home — my spare kicking boots, my punching bag, my dolly . . ."

"YOU have a DOLL?" snorted the Creature.

"Yeah, what of it?" snarled Arabella, clenching her fists. "That dolly was given to me by my grandma on the day she took me in! It means more to me than the boots on my feet! You got a problem with my dolly, you got a problem with me! Well, *do* you?"

"No problem!" said Stitch Head quickly. "The Creature just really likes dolls, too. Right, Creature?"

"They're GREAT! I LOVE them," squeaked the Creature, adding quietly, "PLEASE don't KICK me."

"Right, well, I should go," said Arabella. "Dawn's not for a while — them orphanage folk will have to get up pretty early to catch me. I'll be down and back before they roll into town!"

Stitch Head grinned. "We'll be waiting," he said.

With that, Arabella raced down the corridor toward the Great Door. "Save me a nice room! Preferably one that ain't too burned!"

"It was a — *never mind*," murmured Stitch Head.

THE THIRD CHAPTER

GOODBYE GRUBBERS NUBBIN
(Welcome to your new life)

MAD MUSING No. 116

"Madness is the better
part of science."

From *The Occasionally Scientific
Writings of Professor Erasmus Erasmus*

Arabella couldn't help but smile as she trudged her way back through the snow to Grubbers Nubbin. She had always felt more comfortable in the company of monsters and creations than people, anyway. This was the beginning of a new life, and there was nothing the people from the orphanage could do about it.

She hurried into her house and started packing a bag to take to Castle Grotteskew. She put the bag on her bed, and then reached under her pillow and pulled out her doll. It was surprisingly neat and clean (considering Arabella was anything but) and stylishly dressed in a frilly blue dress and bonnet. She picked up her bag and took a deep breath.

"Bye, Grubbers Nubbin," she said. "And bye, Grandma . . . you crusty old goat."

Arabella walked out of the house into the heavy snow. The streets of Grubbers

Nubbin were deserted and the lamplights extinguished. Arabella made her way down the street, combing her doll's hair and ruffling her own.

She was almost on the outskirts of town when she heard a noise. She turned back to see a horse and carriage crunching through the snow toward her. She slowed to a stop and watched the carriage do the same — directly outside her house. A hunched figure carrying a cane climbed stiffly out of the carriage. He hobbled through the snow to the door and rapped on it with his stick.

"What's going on?" she whispered to herself. She looked at the carriage. In the moonlight, she could just make out the words emblazoned in white upon its side:

OTHERWAYS
Home for Unwanted Orphans

"Can't be . . ." she said, looking up at the moon. "It ain't time yet . . . they've come early!" Then, because she was a Guff through and through (and although she would immediately regret it), she shouted at the top of her voice, "Hey, you cheating, dirty, rot-brained slug! You've come early!"

The old man turned and peered into the gloom.

"Catch me if you can, you stinky pig!" said Arabella. She turned on her heels and ran, dragging her feet through the thick snow as quickly as she could. She looked back to see the old man limping slowly back to the carriage.

Arabella was almost halfway to the castle when she heard the sound of horse's hooves pounding up the hill toward her. The carriage was gaining fast, following the moonlit trail left by her footsteps.

By now the castle obscured the light of the moon. Arabella peered into the inky gloom — and caught sight of the Great Door.

Faster, she thought, *ain't got far to —*

The carriage barreled past her. She leaped out of the way and landed face first in the snow with a *FLOMP*. She picked herself up and dusted the sticky snow off. The carriage slowed to a stop in front of her, blocking her path.

"Filthy rotten goat! You nearly squished me!" Arabella snarled, waving her fist. "I should kick you down this hill and back up again!"

The old man climbed down from the carriage, steadying himself with his stick. "Arabella Guff, I presume? You can always tell the orphans — they're the ones trying to run away in the dead of night," he wheezed. He looked back at the castle. "But where did you think you were going? In there? You wouldn't last five minutes."

"You don't know nothing about me!" growled Arabella. "And you ain't getting me without a fight, pig-hog!"

"Gadsbodkins, you're a rude little urchin, aren't you?" said the old man.

"I'll show you rude, you wrinkly necked, snot-eared snail!" snarled Arabella. "I'll kick your teeth down your stinky neck!"

"I believe you," replied the old man. "It's been a while since I've had the strength to restrain even the smallest youngster."

"Yeah, so back off! I ain't never needed a reason to kick someone!"

"However, I have grown resourceful in my old age," continued the old man. He raised his stick and pointed it directly at Arabella's face. "Don't worry, there's nothing to fear."

Arabella had time to say, "Don't point

that thing at me, you scabby —" before a jet
of thick white gas shot out of the bottom
of the cane. A single gasp of the gas made
Arabella slump limply to the ground, her
doll slipping from her hand into the snow.
The old man took another step forward
and stood over her.

"Welcome to your new life, Arabella
Guff."

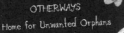

THE FOURTH CHAPTER

TAKEN
(Arabella's doll)

ORPHANS UNDERFOOT?

Waifs, strays, and ragamuffins
are welcome at Otherways Home
for Unwanted Orphans.
Shelter and care offered to
urchins of all shapes and sizes.

Stitch Head had planned to head over to the castle courtyard and wait for Arabella's return . . . but fate had other ideas. One of Professor Erasmus's most recent creations, a horribly hairy bear-wolf named Montague, was afflicted with a sudden bout of Acute Enormity. He had grown so large that he was occupying the castle's whole library.

By the time Stitch Head had mixed and administered a whopping dose of Less Is Best Reduction Remedy, dawn had almost come. With Montague back to a manageable size, Stitch Head joined the Creature and Pox. The three of them hurried to the Great Door to welcome Arabella to her new home.

"HEY, Stitch Head, LOOK! I spent ALL night making a BANNER for ARABELLA! Do you think she'll LIKE it?" asked the Creature. He produced a large roll of fabric from its coat. With a flourish, he unfurled it and let out a deafeningly enthusiastic, "Ta-DA!"

~~HAPY BURTHDAY~~

WELLCOM TO YOR NOO HOME!

(SORRY ABOWT YOR DED GWANDMA)

"It's . . . really heartfelt," said Stitch Head. "But where is Arabella? I thought she would be back from Grubbers Nubbin by n—"

"GRuKK!" barked Pox. He scratched wildly at the door with his claws, leaving little marks in the wood.

"What's the matter with him?" asked Stitch Head.

"He's probably JEALOUS 'cause he

HASN'T made a BANNER . . ." mused the Creature.

Stitch Head pushed a crate right up to the Great Door and climbed on top of it. He peered through the viewing hatch into the slowly lifting gloom.

"All I see is snow," he whispered. He turned the key and carefully pulled open the Great Door. It groaned and rumbled like a snoring giant. Stitch Head held his breath and poked his head into the cold outside.

"Arabella . . . ?" For a moment, Stitch Head thought he heard what sounded like a wagon rolling down the snow-covered hill. Nervously, he inched out of the doorway. "Arabella? Are you there?" He took a few tentative steps outside and spotted a small, dark shape half-buried in the snow. He slowly reached down to pick it up.

It was a doll, slightly squashed and

kind of battered, but nicely dressed in a dress and bonnet. Stitch Head inspected it and found a small, finely embroidered tag threaded to its sleeve. On it were the words:

Arabella,
There's nothing to fear.
I will always take care of you.
Love Grandma xo

Stitch Head's mismatched eyes grew wide.

"BANNER time! WELCOME to your NEW home, Arabella!" began the Creature, emerging from behind the Great Door with its banner half-unrolled. "Hey, WHERE is she?"

"She was here. Arabella was here! Her boot prints are in the snow. Hers and someone else's," said Stitch Head. "Horse's hooves . . . wheel tracks . . . something's wrong — really wrong. Look." Stitch Head held up the doll.

"She DOES look SMALLER than normal," noted the Creature. "And better DRESSED . . ."

"Don't you see? There's no way she'd leave her doll behind!" cried Stitch Head. "They came for her — they've taken her. The people from the orphanage have taken Arabella!"

"Oh, I SEE . . ." said the Creature as the lightbulb went off in his head. "OH NO! ARABELLA!"

"SWaaRTiKi!" howled Pox.

"It's all my fault," said Stitch Head. He cradled Arabella's doll. "If I hadn't been so busy with the bear-wolf, I would have been here waiting for her. I might have heard something, seen something . . ."

"DON'T blame YOURSELF, Stitch Head. If ANYONE is to blame, it's Arabella's GRANDMA for being so DEAD," replied the Creature. "And NOW Arabella has to live in an AWFULAGE where they make her WORK like a WORM and eat dry DOGS . . ."

Stitch Head stared at the doll. "Not if I can help it. We're going to need a plan."

"What KIND of plan?" asked the Creature.

Stitch Head cast his eyes down the hill as dawn began to rise. "A *rescue* plan," he said. "We're going to bring Arabella back."

THE FIFTH CHAPTER

IVO
(The wait for nightfall)

Though we may be monsters all
Here's news to calm your fears,
We never leave these castle walls
(At least we haven't in many years!)

"So what exactly IS the PLAN?" asked the Creature. It and Pox followed Stitch Head down a long, spiral staircase to his dungeon home deep in the bowels of the castle. "I MEAN, we don't even KNOW where they've TAKEN Arabella or ANYTHING . . ."

Stitch Head didn't answer. He pushed open the dungeon door and hurried over to his potion table. A dozen or more test tubes bubbled away — tonics, medicines, and remedies for the (occasionally monstrous) creations of Castle Grotteskew. Stitch Head began filling bottle after bottle with all kinds of pungent, brightly colored liquid.

"Let me HELP!" boomed the Creature. It stamped across the dungeon, knocking a stack of boxes to the floor and breaking Stitch Head's bed in two.

"No! I mean, thanks anyway, but these potions are . . . *very* unstable," Stitch

Head replied. "If the bottles break or the potions mix together, who knows what might happen."

The Creature inched obediently to a corner of the dungeon, and Stitch Head began packing the bottles carefully into a bag. The thought of heading out of his safe castle made his stomach churn. "We'll have to wait for nightfall," he told the Creature. "It's too dangerous in the daylight. Since the fire, the townsfolk are more suspicious than ever. We don't want them forming another angry mob."

Stitch Head put the last of the bottles into his bag and placed Arabella's doll on top. He slung the bag carefully over his shoulder. Then he reached under his broken bed and rifled around.

"What are you LOOKING for?" asked the Creature. "Are you looking for a PLAN?"

"You remember that play you directed,

before the — uh, fire? I managed to save my costume. It's here somewhere . . . aha!"

Stitch Head pulled out a bundle of clothes and unwrapped them. Within moments he was wearing trousers, a jacket, and a wide, flat cap. They were all too large for him, but he did appear more human than usual.

"How do I look?" he asked.

"SWaRTiKi!" barked Pox.

"Yeah, GREAT!" boomed the Creature, saluting with all three hands. "BUT where's MY costume?"

Stitch Head stared up at the Creature. It blinked its single eye and swished its tail expectantly.

"Creature, I'm sorry," Stitch Head said with a sigh. "You can't come with me."

"WHAT an ADVENTURE! Next stop, the AWFULAGE!" the Creature continued obliviously.

"It's just — we can't afford to draw attention to ourselves," continued Stitch Head.

"I can't WAIT to see the LOOK on Arabella's FACE when we show up and RESCUE her! She'll be ALL, 'No WAY! You RESCUED me! AND you made me a BANNER' — Wait, WHAT?"

"I'm sorry," began Stitch Head. "It's just that — and please don't take this the wrong way — you're not exactly *inconspicuous*."

"WHOA . . . Is THIS about my PUTTING on WEIGHT?" cried the Creature, taken aback. "Don't PRETEND you haven't NOTICED . . ."

"What? No, you look great, I just —"

"Stitch Head, PLEASE! I'll be as UNCONSPICUOUS as a MOUSE! And not those GLOW-IN-THE-DARK mice that LIVE in the castle PANTRY . . ."

"Look, who else is going to supervise the repairs to the castle?" added Stitch Head quickly. "You're a born foreman! Well, a *created* foreman . . . and someone's got to hold down the fort, look after Professor Erasmus, and keep everything running smoothly. I can't think of anyone better qualified than you."

"I SUPPOSE . . . I mean, I DO

command a certain RESPECT around here," the Creature replied, flexing its muscles a little. "But there's no WAY you're going out there into the big, WILD world all ALONE. SOMEONE'S got to watch your BACKPACK. What about POX?"

"GruKK!" barked the monkey-bat.

"Uh, maybe. But what about the whole brutally-attacking-everyone-he-meets thing?" whispered Stitch Head.

"GOOD point," agreed the Creature. "Then WHO?"

Stitch Head's eyes widened. "I think I know . . . and I know just where to find him."

Moments later, the Creature and Pox were trying to keep up with Stitch Head as he hurried up the winding staircases of Grotteskew. They climbed higher and higher until they found themselves on what remained of the castle parapet.

"WHAT are we DOING up HERE?" asked the Creature, peering into the sky.

"There's only one other creation who might just pass for almost-human," replied Stitch Head. "The first creation of Grotteskew."

"WHAT? I thought YOU were the first — Oh, WAIT, you mean IVO, the professor's DAD'S first creation? WHAT would HE be doing all the WAY up HERE?"

"Stitch Head! You have to look at this!" came a cry. A tiny, oval head poked over the highest parapet. "I can see whole *world* from up here!"

Ivo was the first creation to be "born" in Grotteskew, created by Professor Erasmus's father, the confusingly named Professor Erasmus. He was a small, frail-looking creature. His slender frame was dressed in rags, and he had a single, spindly metal arm.

Next to him, even Stitch Head looked like a giant.

"You see that cloud in sky? Cloud is shaped like tree!" Ivo squeaked excitedly as Stitch Head and the Creature joined him on the parapet. "And down there in field, snow-covered tree looks like cloud! Mad science is smart, but nature is miracles! I stand here on top of castle and I wonder, what is out there in big, wide world?"

"Do you want to find out?" replied Stitch Head. "Arabella's been taken to live in an orphanage. Will you help me get her back?"

"Angry Girl gone? I help, of course!" agreed Ivo. "Angry Girl is good friend. She help me when I need help — well, mainly she kick me, but her heart is in right place. So what is plan to rescue Angry Girl?"

Stitch Head looked out over the big, wide world. "I'll tell you when I think of one."

LINES IN THE SNOW
(The journey)

MAD MUSING No. 707

"To laugh is human —
to cackle is divine."

From *The Occasionally Scientific
Writings of Professor Erasmus Erasmus*

As dusk began to fall and cover things with a dark gloominess, Stitch Head made his way to the professor's laboratory. He had to be sure his master wasn't about to awaken any new creations that might need curing of their monstrousness. He sat in his usual place in the rafters, peering down as his master worked madly on some half-finished horror.

"AAaAHA! I know I've said it before, but this will be my greatest creation ever!" cackled the professor, with an arm in one hand and a tentacle in the other. "Ever, ever! AHAa AHAaHAAAA!"

Stitch Head shrugged and let out a long sigh. He had long ago given up trying to get his master to remember him. All the professor ever cared about was his next creation. He hadn't even noticed that half the castle had almost burned down around him. Anyway, Stitch Head had bigger things to worry about. Arabella wasn't going to rescue herself . . . probably.

"See you soon, master," he said, getting to his feet. "I hope."

Stitch Head hurried down to the courtyard where Ivo, the Creature, and Pox were waiting. Together they pulled open the Great Door.

"Take care of things while we're away, Creature," said Stitch Head.

"Don't WORRY, the castle's in safe HANDS — all THREE of THEM," boomed the Creature.

Stitch Head smiled. "We'll be back in no time . . . *with* Arabella."

He pulled his jacket around him and tugged down his cap.

"How come you get to dress like chimney sweep, but I do not get disguise?" huffed Ivo, pulling his cloak of rags over his head as they stepped outside into the snow.

"Honestly? I couldn't find anything in your size," replied Stitch Head. "But we'll think of something."

+‍+

Stitch Head and Ivo made their way down the hill. Their feet disappeared in the thick snow, and their breaths puffed out of their mouths in clouds. As they followed the carriage's tracks, the freezing air clawed at their faces.

"Snow is miracles! Like whole world has been painted!" exclaimed Ivo. The little creation was waist deep in snow, trying to keep up with Stitch Head.

"Um, it might be better if we stay *quiet*," whispered Stitch Head as they passed by the outskirts of Grubbers Nubbin. Stitch Head had grown to fear the townsfolk as much as they feared the castle. Humans were unpredictable, and there wasn't a potion in the world that could cure them of that. As they ventured out into the unknown, Stitch Head longed for the safety of Grotteskew's dark corners.

"Why do we not get humans of Grubbers Nubbin to help us look for Arabella?" asked Ivo as they crept past the town. "They are not conspicuous like three-armed monsters and savage monkey-bats."

Stitch Head almost laughed at the thought of it. "It doesn't work like that, Ivo," he replied. "Humans and creations are different. We just don't mix."

"I see," nodded Ivo. "Except we go to rescue Angry Girl. Angry Girl is human."

"Yeah, well, I'm pretty sure

Arabella isn't like other humans," said Stitch Head. "Come on. The tracks lead down the road."

━━━━━━━━━━━━━━━━━━━━━━━

Stich Head and Ivo walked through the night, following the trail — up rolling hills, down deep valleys, and past sleeping towns. They had both spent an almost-lifetime in the shadows. But while Ivo saw this new world as a vast, white canvas of possibility, all Stitch Head saw were countless dangers.

Rays of morning sun were starting to hit the white snow, which sparkled in the soft light. "We should find somewhere to lie low," Stitch Head said. He picked up speed as they followed the tracks up a long, tree-lined road. "We'll start again at nightfall."

"Perhaps we hide in that big house?" suggested Ivo.

"Big house?" At the end of the road, in the pale morning light, stood a wide, towering building. It was much larger and more imposing than anything Stitch Head had ever seen in Grubbers Nubbin. It stood peacefully, majestically — as if it belonged there.

"The tracks lead that way," added Stitch Head, continuing cautiously down the road. Sure enough, outside the house was a large, black carriage. Stitch Head moved closer until he could make out a sign emblazoned on its side.

OTHERWAYS
Home for Unwanted Orphans

"It's an orphanage," said Stitch Head. "This has to be the place! We've *found* it!"

"Now we stage daring rescue, yes?" asked Ivo. "We storm in and shout, 'We are monsters! We eat your brains for breakfast and your spleen for a snack!' And then we rescue Arabella, yes?"

"Uh, something like that," said Stitch Head with a shrug.

THE SEVENTH CHAPTER

DISGUISES
(Getting through the door)

Creations and humans do not mix,
This is our rule of thumb.
Feel free to try it, if you wish,
But it may not be much fun.

Stitch Head inched nervously toward the front door. He fastened his coat and pulled the cap down on his head.

In the right light, I just might pass as human, he thought. But Ivo, with his miniscule frame and metal arm, was a different matter. Stitch Head searched in his bag again. "Wait a minute, why didn't I think of this before?"

Stitch Head pulled Arabella's doll out of his bag and held it up against Ivo. They were almost exactly the same size.

"I think I am not wanting to do this," said Ivo immediately.

Three minutes later, Ivo was dressed in a flamboyantly frilly blue dress, complete with lace trim and an attractive bonnet. Stitch Head put Arabella's doll back into his bag.

"This is *humiliating*," said Ivo.

"It's the perfect cover — I'm a wretched

orphan and you're my only possession," assured Stitch Head. He took Ivo's hand. "All you need to do is play dead. I mean, play *doll*. I mean . . . just don't move a muscle."

"Next time, *you* get to be the doll," huffed Ivo, slumping lifelessly into the snow.

Stitch Head held his breath and reached slowly for the bell. Finally, he pulled the cord and they heard a loud chime ring from inside.

"No one home? Oh well, let's try new plan," whispered Ivo.

"No visitors!" came a cry as the door swung open. There stood a crooked old man in a crumpled suit and black tie. Adorning the tie was a polished silver tie clip in the shape of a spider. Stitch Head pulled his cap further down on his head and stared at the snow.

"Gadsbodkins! Not another wretched runt begging for a free dinner? Begone, before I tell your parents you're a filthy beggar!"

"Uh, I don't have any parents," muttered Stitch Head, improvising. "I'm an orphan."

"Rot and gobbledygook! That's what they all say, only to return to their family once they've eaten their fill!" snarled the old man. "*If* you are an orphan, what happened to your parents?"

Stitch Head kicked himself for not thinking of a story before he rang the doorbell.

"They were, um . . . eaten?"

"*Eaten?*" the old man asked.

"By a bear-wolf!" replied a panicking Stitch Head. "I mean wolf! I mean bear!"

"Ridiculous! Do you think I was born yesterday?" barked the old man, jabbing Stitch Head with his cane. Stitch Head fell back into the snow, and his cap fell from his head. He scrabbled around in the snow to put it back on, but, for a split second, his eyes met with the old man's.

"Gadzooks!" the old man cried.

Stitch Head jammed his cap back on and grabbed Ivo. He glanced up to see the

old man shaking like a leaf. Stitch Head wondered if his stitches made him look even more hideous than he thought.

"The, uh, bear got me, too," he said quickly.

"You . . ." muttered the old man, still shaking, sweat beading on his brow. "What are . . . you . . . *doing* here?"

Stitch Head wasn't sure he understood the question, so he just said, "I-I'm an orphan . . ."

The old man composed himself. He straightened his tie and stood as upright as his old body would allow.

"Very well," he replied. "If that's the way you want to play it."

With that, he pulled Stitch Head through the door and slammed it shut.

THE EIGHTH CHAPTER

WELCOME TO OTHERWAYS
(Bienvenue à Otherways)

There will always be an
OTHERWAYS

The old man dragged Stitch Head inside and steadied himself with his stick.

Stitch Head looked up. They were in a bright, open hall with high ceilings and gleaming chandeliers. The floor was polished hardwood, and half a dozen large windows seemed to invite the sunlight inside. A curved stairway led up from the center of the room. It was far grander than anything he'd ever seen before. There was a distinct smell of roses, home cooking, and a fire. It was so perfectly warm that Stitch Head's skin began to tingle. It was as far from the scorched gloom of Castle Grotteskew as was possible.

"Um, excuse me," began Stitch Head, gripping Ivo tightly. He kept his cap as low as he could. "I'm looking for —"

"I know what you're looking for, but I can assure you, you won't find it here," hissed the old man. He took out a pocket watch from inside his jacket. Stitch Head noticed that it, too, was adorned with a silver spider. "It's almost time . . ."

"Time for what?" asked Stitch Head nervously.

From every corner of the hall, from every doorway and corridor, there appeared children. One after the other they came — children of all ages, shapes, and sizes. Each one was immaculately dressed in clean, well-pressed, matching uniforms. Everyone's hair was neatly combed to the same side and their shoes shined like mirror. There must have been a hundred of them. They filed silently into the hall without even looking at each other. Finally, in effortless unison, the children stopped and turned to face the large staircase.

"I don't see Arabella," Stitch Head whispered to Ivo. He decided that if his disguise was enough to fool the old man, perhaps it would work on the children as well. He took a deep breath and dared to tap the nearest child on the elbow (as high as he could reach). The boy slowly turned to face him. He did not seem in the least bit horrified by Stitch Head's appearance. In

fact, he seemed quite distant, as if he were somewhere else entirely.

"Ex-excuse me," whispered Stitch Head. "I'm looking for my friend."

The boy stared at him without emotion, his eyes glassy and vague.

"She's, um, she's a human — I mean,

she's a girl," he began. "She's about your height . . . maybe taller. She's got, um, some hair and a face . . . and kicking boots! You'd remember her if you met her."

The boy lifted his finger to his lips and made a soft "Shhhhh." Then he turned back to face the staircase. A moment later, Stitch Head heard an odd, unfamiliar sound.

It was the sound of singing.

Non! Les parents, les parents

Non! Qui a besoin de parents?

Stitch Head didn't understand a word, but the tune was haunting and melodious, the voice as bright as sunshine. At the top of the stairs, silhouetted against the morning light, a figure emerged.

"*Mes enfants . . .* my children!"

As the figure moved slowly, gracefully down the stairs, Stitch Head realized it was a human woman. She was slender and tall, with a rising curl of perfectly arranged hair, and she was dressed entirely in black. Her great domed skirt reached to the floor. Stitch Head could not help but gasp. She was more beautiful than anything he had ever seen.

"*Bonjour mes petits* — how it warms my 'eart to 'ave you 'ere with me, as if you were

my own sons and daughters," the woman said, her voice soft and wooing. "But tell me, my orphans — are you 'appy?"

"Yes, Madame Venin," replied the children together in a cool monotone.

"*Bon!* Zen if you are 'appy, *I* am 'appy! Zis is the way at Otherways — we are *une famille* — a family! And — wait, what is zis? A stranger in our midst?" Somehow, through the huge crowd of children, she had fixed her gaze upon Stitch Head.

"Uh-oh," he whispered, squeezing Ivo's metal arm.

"Doctor, you did not tell me we 'ad a new addition," she said, looking to the old man.

"Gracious Madame," replied the old man, his eyes wide in hypnotic admiration. "This one is . . . new. He says a bear claimed his parents and left him worse for wear — as you can see."

"I see only a child in need of care, Doctor," replied Madame Venin. "*Mon petit,* let me 'ave a look at you."

The crowd of children parted in unison. Stitch Head gulped as Madame Venin glided elegantly and across the large hall toward him.

"Tragedy is ze beginning of every story at Otherways," she began. "Your parents' untimely demise is in ze past. Zis is your future. Tell me, child, what is your name?"

"Uh . . . Stanley," replied Stitch Head.

"Stanley, you are safe now," assured Madame Venin, placing her hand gently upon Stitch Head's small shoulder. "Soon, all your loneliness and sadness and fear will disappear. Soon you will learn it is not so awful to be an orphan. Am I right, *mes petits*?"

"Yes, Madame Venin," droned the children.

"*Oui!* Of course I am right! Now take it away!"

"Take what away?" asked Stitch Head. All of a sudden, the children began clicking their fingers in perfect, passionless unison. Something strange was happening.

Stitch Head could feel a song coming on.

THE MYSTIQUE OF MADAME VENIN

(A song and dance)

It's Not So Awful Being an Orphan

Une Composition Originale de Madame Venin

Stitch Head watched, open-mouthed, as Madame Venin broke into exuberant song. She strode around, accompanied by finger clicking and measured (if emotionless) humming from the children.

It's not so awful being an orphan,
For parents are a drag,
A father's such a bother
And a mother is a nag.

It's not so awful being an orphan,
You're not ruled by Ma or Pa,
Do as you please, mes petits —
It's better 'ere, by far!

Why, you'd rather be an orphan
When your life is not your own.
Do zis! Do zat! And tidy up!
You're a slave in your own 'ome.

If only you could find a way
To escape ze drudgery!
To slip your parents' clutches
And to finally be free!

It's not so awful being an orphan,
In fact, it's rather nice,
Young Henry likes it so much
Zat he's been orphaned twice!

Stanley, your life's not ended
Because you lost your père et mère
It's the beginning of a new life,
So be thankful for zat bear!

Madame Venin bowed deeply and the children immediately began to clap. The doctor applauded too — so excitedly that he looked like he might collapse. Stitch Head glanced down at Ivo, who dared to open an eye.

"Any sign of Angry Girl?" Ivo whispered.

"Not yet," replied Stitch Head. It suddenly occurred to him that if anyone was going to make their presence known at Otherways, it was Arabella. Perhaps she had decided not to stay . . .

"Too kind, *mes petits*, too kind," cooed Madame Venin. "Well, all zis singing 'as given me an appetite! Let us eat!"

Dried worms, thought Stitch Head, remembering Arabella's warning. *Maybe I'll just pretend I'm not hungry.*

Stitch Head followed the children, Madame Venin, and a glaring doctor through the door at the end of the hall.

The room was huge and grand. On the walls hung fine paintings of glorious landscapes, and in the center of the room was an incredibly long table. It was laid out with plate after plate of colorful, sweet-smelling food — freshly baked bread, cakes, pastries, and bright, perfectly ripe fruit. It was far more than even this small army of children could consume. It was an unfeasibly sumptuous feast — as far from dried worms as you could get.

"What are you waiting for?" laughed Madame Venin. "Dig in, my orphans!"

Stitch Head did not need food to survive — but he decided that to maintain his cover (and because his mouth had started to water) he should join in. He crawled up onto a chair next to Madame Venin, placed Ivo and his bag gently on the floor, and then ate like he had never eaten before (which he hadn't).

"I love to cook for my children! I love to see zem 'appy!" cried Madame Venin. Stitch Head greedily finished off his third chocolate cream doughnut.

Even Arabella couldn't complain about this, he thought. But she was never a fan of singing. Still, Stitch Head concluded, even if she had come and gone from the orphanage, she was not an easy person to forget. He wiped his mouth and turned to Madame Venin.

"Um, Madame?" he began. "Do you know a girl called Arabella?"

"Is she a friend of yours, Stanley?" replied Madame Venin. "Is she an orphan?"

"Um, yes," said Stitch Head.

"Then she is always welcome at Otherways." Madame Venin placed her hands upon her heart. "We will gladly take 'er in — I will care for 'er as if she were a member of my own family."

"I was sure she'd be here . . ." muttered Stitch Head, glancing down at Ivo. Did they have the right place? Could they have taken a wrong turn and ended up at a different orphanage?

"Per'aps you will see 'er soon. Those who 'ave nowhere else to go tend to find us," said Madame Venin with a warm smile.

"But tell me, Stanley, 'ave you eaten your fill of *petit déjeuner?*

"What? Oh, the food!" replied Stitch Head. "Yes, thank you. I've never eaten before — I mean, I've never eaten so *much* before."

"Well, you're a growing boy, after all — let us 'ope!" noted Madame Venin. "Come then, let us begin ze day."

"Is it time to work?" asked Stitch Head, adding a nervous, "*Like dogs?*" under his breath.

"Work? Ze very idea. *Non*, my orphans may do as zey please!" laughed Madame Venin. "You never 'ave to do another day's work in your life!"

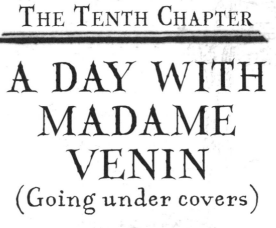

THE TENTH CHAPTER

A DAY WITH MADAME VENIN

(Going under covers)

Who needs parents, anyway? Zey really are a bind.
So if zey meet a sorry end, you shouldn't really mind.
Who needs parents, anyway? Why, death comes to them all!
If it comes a little sooner, zen why worry? 'Ave a ball!

From Who Needs Parents, Anyway?

Une Composition Originale de Madame Venin

Stitch Head looked on as the children of Otherways withdrew from the dining room. He picked up Ivo and his bag, and followed Madame Venin into the hall. The children immediately split up and disappeared down corridors, up the stairs, or into other rooms.

"Where are they going?" asked Stitch Head quietly.

"Zey go where zey please," Madame Venin chuckled. "Zey go to sit in silence and stillness."

"Huh," said Stitch Head. "Don't they want to play?"

"I 'ave never and will never tell *mes enfants* what to do. Zey do as zey please," she replied. "What pleases zem is doing nothing."

Stitch Head poked his head around a door, to see a little boy staring out of the window, silent and unmoving. It seemed out of place, but to Stitch Head it wasn't that strange — after all, he'd spent *years* in the castle without moving an inch, waiting in vain for the professor to remember him. He had to admit, it was *peaceful*.

Perhaps, he thought, that's why Arabella doesn't like orphanages. She never did anything peacefully — she was always shouting and kicking.

"And what would you like to do, Stanley?" asked Madame Venin.

Stitch Head glanced down at the disguised Ivo. "Maybe . . . a tour?"

╾┼┼┼┼┼┼┼┼┼╼╾┼╾┼┼┼┼┼┼┼┼┼┼┼╼╾

Stitch Head and Ivo spent the day with Madame Venin. She gave her new friend "Stanley" a thorough tour of the house (singing to him constantly), giving him the chance to inspect every room (except for the doctor's study, which was locked). Every now and again, Stitch Head would spot the doctor spying on them from behind a door or through a window. Though he felt sure that Madame Venin had bought their disguises, he was starting to worry about the doctor.

As they toured the garden, the gloom of dusk started to settle all around them. "Madame Venin," asked Stitch Head, "who, um, brings the orphans here? I saw a horse and carriage outside the house . . ."

"Why, ze doctor brings all of my lovely children safely to Otherways," Madame Venin replied.

"And if . . . if an orphan didn't want to stay?" Stitch Head asked.

Madame Venin stopped by an old well that was overgrown with plants and dry roots. "Do you wish to leave, Stanley?"

"What? Oh, no!" Stitch Head replied. "It's just . . . my friend . . ."

"When I feel a little lost, Stanley, do you know what I do? I make a wish." Madame Venin took two coins out of a pocket in her dress. She tossed one into the well. It plinked and clinked down the hole.

"Make a wish, Stanley," she said, handing Stitch Head the other coin. He looked out over the garden and saw moonlight dancing across a wide, frozen lake.

Stitch Head threw the coin into the well. "I wish —"

"*Non*, do not tell me or ze wish will not come true." She smiled. "Zere is no 'arm in keeping a secret or two. Now zen, 'ow about supper?"

Despite his concerns, Stitch Head still managed to gorge himself for the third time that day. He stifled a burp as the children stood up all at once and wished Madame Venin a good night before taking themselves to bed. Stitch Head faked a yawn, picked up Ivo, and followed them upstairs to the dormitory.

The room was filled with one hundred beds lined up in neat rows. The children were already asleep, their chests rising and falling in unison as they slept. Stitch Head carried Ivo to an empty bed, clambered in, and pulled the covers over them.

"This place *weird*," said Ivo immediately. "Why children sit around and do nothing all day?"

"I think it's sort of . . . peaceful," Stitch Head whispered, taking off his cap.

"Being dragged along ground in lacy dress for hours is not so peaceful," grumbled Ivo, adjusting his bonnet. "Why do we spend whole day with orphanage lady instead of searching for Angry Girl?"

"I *was* looking for her! I thought a tour would be a good way to look around."

"*I* think you have *crush* on orphanage lady," Ivo said with a grin.

"I do not have a — look, that's beside the point. Where is Arabella?"

"Maybe she decide she does not like weird place full of weird children who do not do things and lady who sings all the —" Ivo paused. "Wait, do you hear sound? I hear sound. Is it singing? I am so sick of singing . . ."

"I don't hear anything," replied Stitch Head.

"It sound like . . . cry for help."

"Who'd cry for help here?"

"Listen!" said Ivo, pulling the covers off their heads. All Stitch Head could hear was the unnervingly uniform breathing of the children.

"You must have imagined it," he whispered. I don't hear a —"

"*Get away!*"

"Okay, that I heard," Stitch Head replied, a shiver running down his back and back up again. "It sounds like — like —"

"*I said get away from me, rotten scum-breath!*"

Stitch Head's eyes grew wide. "Arabella!"

THE SECRET PASSAGE
(Webs in the walls)

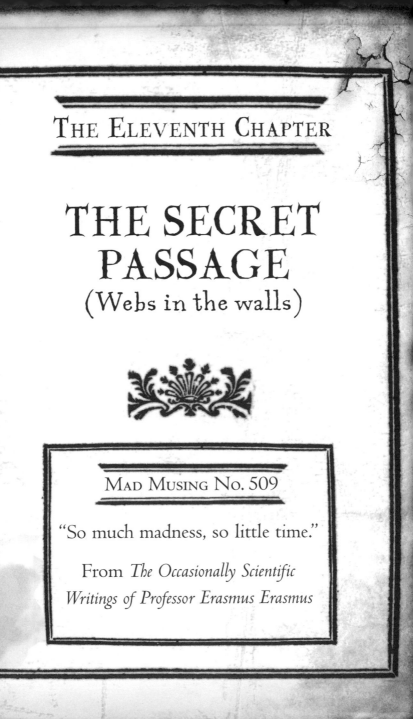

MAD MUSING No. 509

"So much madness, so little time."

From *The Occasionally Scientific Writings of Professor Erasmus Erasmus*

"*S*tick it up your nostrils, boil-brain!"

"Arabella, I'm coming!" Stitch Head cried. He leaped out of bed and raced out of the dormitory. Ivo hitched up his skirt and hurried after him.

"Wait for me!" Ivo cried. "Doll clothing hard to run in!"

"It's coming from downstairs — this way!" said Stitch Head. He ran down the stairs and into the hall. He stopped for a moment, tilting his head to hear.

"*I'll kick you into next week!*"

"The dining room!" said Stich Head and dashed inside . . . but the room was empty. "Where is she? Why is she crying out? She must be close — I can hear her! Arabella! Where are you?"

"*I'll twist off your legs, dirt-face!*"

"How can we hear her if she not here? Is like she is in walls!" said a desperate Ivo.

"In the walls . . . ?" repeated Stitch Head.

He made his way urgently around the room, reaching up and tapping one painting after another with his fingers.

"Maybe this not best time to become admirer of art," suggested Ivo.

"There are secret passages all over Castle Grotteskew — shortcuts and hidden chambers. What if . . ." Stitch Head trailed off as he came to an imposing landscape of (as it happened) a dark, foreboding castle. He tapped it gently, and then slid his tiny fingers around the frame. After a moment there came a click and the painting slid sideways across the wall.

"Ivo, *look*," whispered Stitch Head.

A long, dark passageway stretched out before them, as shadowy as any in Grotteskew and filled with thick, dusty cobwebs.

"What we do?" squeaked a nervous Ivo. "I have bad feeling about this . . ."

"These cobwebs have been broken," said Stitch Head, brushing his fingers gently across the webs. "Someone's been down here recently."

Ivo sighed. "We are going to go down there, aren't we?"

The passage was impenetrably dark — even Stitch Head was having a hard time adjusting to the gloom.

"How come is it that we always end up in very dark places?" muttered Ivo. "Especially with spiders. I have phobia, you know . . ."

"Wait, you're scared of spiders?" said Stitch Head. "But you live in a dark, forbidding castle. There are spiders in every nook and cranny . . ."

"It is *phobia*," repeated Ivo. "I do not like the way they scuttle. And also when they are still. And also everything else about them. They make certain patches of my skin crawl."

"There's nothing to fear," Stitch Head replied. "They're more afraid of you than you are of — OW!"

He had stepped on something sharp. He reached down, pulled it out of his foot, and held it up to get a closer look.

It was a small, silver tie clip shaped like a spider.

"The doctor . . ." said Stitch Head, slipping the pin into his pocket. "He must have been down here!"

"*Lemme alone, you ugly — mmff!*"

"We're getting closer! Come on!" cried Stitch Head.

Stitch Head broke into a sprint. Ivo did his best to hobble after him.

"Wait! Do not leave me with spiders!"

"I can see light! We're — *AHH!*"

For a second, it was as though the ground had disappeared from under his feet. Then Stitch Head felt himself sliding down a slope.

He stuck out his arms to steady himself against the walls, but just ended up with handfuls of webs. A patch of dim light appeared in front of him. A moment later Stitch Head landed with a *THUD!* on cold, hard stone.

"Oww . . ." he muttered. He stood up and dusted himself off. "What happ—"

"Please look out below!" came a cry.

Stitch Head turned around just as Ivo barreled into him, sending them both crumpling to the ground.

"My dress is all dusty," groaned Ivo, scrambling to his feet. "Also, thank you for breaking my fall."

"No — ow — problem," replied Stitch Head, rubbing his head as he got to his feet. "What is this place?"

They were in a wide, dimly lit chamber, illuminated by moonlight from a small hole in the ceiling high above them. Behind them were two openings in the wall. One led back up into the secret passage, the other into inky darkness. And covering every surface . . .

"More webs," shivered Ivo. "I think there is good chance we see spider."

"Spiders won't hurt you," replied Stitch Head. "I'm more worried about —"

"*Mmmf! Mmmmf!*"

Stitch Head spun around. At the other end of the chamber was a web like no other. It was vast — stretching from floor to ceiling and wall-to-wall. Each thread was as thick as string and glinted with stickiness. It took Stitch Head a moment to realize there was something in the center of the web. And then a moment longer to realize it was not something . . . but someone.

"Arabella!" Stitch Head cried.

Arabella was bound in a cocoon of webbing. Only the top of her head and one of her kicking boots could be seen. Even her mouth was covered.

"Mmmf!" she said, shaking with rage. "Mmmf-mf-mmf!"

"Is that . . . giant spider's web?" squeaked Ivo. "I still have bad feeling about this."

"Hang on! We'll get you down!" cried Stitch Head. He raced over to the great web and started to climb up the taut, gummy strands.

"Gmff, mmff! Gmmf!" replied Arabella as Stitch Head reached her and tried to pull the webbing apart.

"I think that she's trying to tell us something!" said Stitch Head. He pulled with all his might, tugging the webbing from Arabella's mouth.

"What happened, Arabella? Are you all right?"

"Run . . ." Arabella said between gasps. "RUN!"

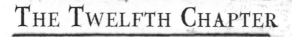

THE TWELFTH CHAPTER

THE SPIDER'S LAIR
(Run!)

MAD MUSING No. 87

"What others call the Impossibly
Terrifying Creation of a Twisted Mad
Genius, I call Tuesday afternoon."

From *The Occasionally Scientific
Writings of Professor Erasmus Erasmus*

"I said RUN!" cried Arabella.

"We're not going anywhere! We're here to rescue you!" replied Stitch Head, trying to free her from the cocoon of webbing. "What happened? Who did this to you?"

"Sp-sp-spider!" blurted Ivo.

"Ivo, I told you, a tiny little spider's not going to do you any harm," said Stitch Head. "Now help get Arabella down from this giant . . . spider's . . . web . . . Uh-oh."

Stitch Head slowly turned around. At the other end of the chamber he saw a long, spindly leg thrust out from the dark opening in the wall and onto the floor. Then came another leg, and another — appendage after appendage, stretching like shadows across the chamber. Within moments, the shape of a colossal, monstrous spider emerged. It was obscured by shadow, but Stitch Head could see that it was almost as big as the Creature. Its curved abdomen glistened in the dim light, and its eight long legs arced out from its body, disappearing into dark corners.

"Worthless rot-breath boil-brain! You don't scare me! I've seen bigger spiders in my grandma's basement!" cried Arabella.

"This may not be the best time to aggravate the giant spider," whispered Stitch Head. He looked back to see a motionless Ivo, the spider looming over him.

"Ivo, move!" shouted Stitch Head.

"I cannot," replied Ivo. "Phobia has left me frozen with fear. Please to help!"

Stitch Head turned back to Arabella. "I'll be back! Wait here!"

"Where am I going to go?" snorted Arabella.

Stitch Head leaped to the floor. He had tackled many menacing monsters in the past, but they had all been the creation of Professor Erasmus Erasmus. What was this new horror? Instinctively he reached for his bag of potions, but he had left it under the bed.

"Um, leave him alone!" shouted Stitch Head, racing toward the spider.

With a flick of an enormous leg, the

spider sent Ivo crashing into a wall and lunged at Stitch Head. As it flew toward him, Stitch Head got his first look at the spider's massive, seesawing jaws and sharp fangs. He ducked and skidded under its great legs, but the spider wheeled around with breathtaking speed. It batted him along the ground with a leg, sending him skittering across the cold stone floor.

"Stitch Head!" cried Arabella as the spider scuttled toward him. Stitch Head scrabbled around for anything to use as

a weapon, when he remembered . . . the doctor's tie clip!

He reached into his pocket, the spider's jaws inches from his face. He caught sight of a glossy black eye and jabbed the tie clip into it as hard as he could.

SKREEEEEE!

The spider reared up in pain. Stitch Head leaped to his feet once more, but the spider had already recovered. It grabbed him in its jaws and flung him across the room. Stitch Head saw the wall quickly approaching . . .

Then the world went black.

THE THIRTEENTH CHAPTER

THE NIGHTMARE SCENARIO

(Nothing to fear)

MAD MUSING No. 219

"A nightmare is just a monster
I haven't made yet."

From *The Occasionally Scientific
Writings of Professor Erasmus Erasmus*

"Spider!" Stitch Head sat up with a start. He was back in his bed in the orphanage dormitory. The room was empty. Sparkling dust danced in the morning light, and a sharp breeze pinched his skin. He checked himself to make sure he was still in one piece.

"Ivo?" He looked around the bed, then under it. There was no sign of Ivo . . . and his potion bag was missing.

"What? Where?" he murmured, before he heard the sound of singing.

Non! Les parents, les parents

Non! Qui a besoin de parents?

The doors to the dormitory swung open. Stitch Head quickly searched under his covers for his cap, but it was nowhere to be seen. He pulled the covers up to his face as Madame Venin swept into the room, closely followed by the limping doctor.

"Stanley! You are awake! *Merveilleux!*"

cried Madame Venin, gliding across the room toward him. Before he knew it, she was standing over him, her hands pressed together. "How do you feel? Are you quite well? You are still very pale . . ."

"It'll take a miracle to put color back in this grimy urchin's cheeks," sneered the doctor.

"Poor Stanley, you gave us quite a fright, with all zat screaming and 'ollering," said Madame Venin softly.

"Screaming? I wasn't screaming — I *heard* screaming . . ." said Stitch Head.

"But you 'ad a nightmare, *mon petit*," Madame Venin replied. "You fell into a deep sleep and 'ad a bad dream. Apparently you were crying out so loudly zat you woke ze other orphans . . ."

"What? No, it was —" Stitch Head began.

"Ze doctor said it was best to let you

sleep, but we could not 'elp but 'ear you crying out about *un monstre* — a monster," continued Madame Venin.

Stitch Head quickly stole a glance at the doctor's tie.

His tie clip — it's missing!

"Madame Venin, you have to believe me. I didn't have a nightmare," Stitch Head insisted. "There's something terrible here. I heard screaming, and I found a secret passage and I —"

"Horse feathers!" the doctor huffed. "This child is delusional. He should be in an asylum, not an orphanage."

"Can you not see, Doctor, zat Stanley is distressed by 'is nightmare?" said Madame Venin.

"It wasn't a nightmare!" insisted Stitch Head again. "There was a giant spider, as big as a man!"

"Stanley, you must try to calm down," concluded Madame Venin. "We are all 'ere to take care of you. We are your family — me, ze doctor . . ."

"There's nothing to fear . . ." said the doctor, inching closer.

"No! I-I'll prove it! I'll show you!" cried Stitch Head. He leaped out of bed and raced out of the room.

"Stanley! *Reviens!* Come back!" cried Madame Venin.

Stitch Head ran downstairs, through the

hall and into the dining room, where the other children were having breakfast. Their heads turned slowly as he rushed to the painting of the castle. He slid his fingers behind the frame and frantically felt for the secret catch.

"Where is it?" he muttered, lifting the corner of the painting and peering behind the frame. *"Where is it?"*

He pulled the frame as hard as he could, dragging it off the wall. It fell to the floor with a *BUMP!* Stitch Head's eyes widened in horror. There was no passageway — the wall behind the painting was intact and untouched. It was simply a wall.

"It wasn't like this! There was a dark corridor and cobwebs . . . there was a giant spider!" The children stared at him with nothing but disinterest in their eyes. A frustrated Stitch Head rushed into the kitchen and out the back door.

"Arabella! Ivo!" he shouted, stumbling down the garden through the snow. He heard Madame Venin calling, "Stanley!" behind him. But he did not want to be found — not yet — not before he'd tried to make sense of what was happening and come up with a plan. He spied the well at the end of the garden and ducked behind it, huddling in the snow and staring out over the frozen lake.

He noticed a figure kneeling by the shore. It was one of the orphans — a girl. She was motionless, peering at the ice. What was she doing out here in the cold? The orphans never seemed to leave the house. Stitch Head got to his feet and walked over to her. He held his breath and tapped her on the shoulder.

The girl turned to face him. She was dressed identically to all the other children, with neat, starched clothing and carefully combed hair. It took Stitch Head a moment to realize who it was . . .

"Arabella!"

Arabella stared at him. She had a distant look in her eye — as if she were somewhere else entirely. It was the exact same expression that was on the face of every child in the orphanage.

After a moment she smiled weakly, the tiniest flash of recognition in her eyes. "Oh," she began, her voice flat and emotionless. "Hello, Stanley."

THE FOURTEENTH CHAPTER

LOOKING FOR ARABELLA
(Lost in the Snow)

Oh, to be an orphan, what a life zat life would be.
To do exactly as I wanted, to be absolutely free!
If I became an orphan, it would be une bonne surprise!
So shuffle off, you parents! Farewell! Begone! Demise!

From Oh, to be an Orphan
Une Composition Originale de Madame Venin

"Arabella, you're all right!" cried Stitch Head. "What happened? What are you doing out here? How did you escape?"

"Why would I want to escape, Stanley?" she replied flatly. "Everything I need is here at the orphanage."

Stitch Head felt a little shiver run down his spine.

"Arabella, it's me! It's Stitch Head!" he said, grabbing her by the shoulders. "Where's Ivo? Why are you dressed like that?"

"Madame Venin lets us dress however we like," she said coolly.

"But you — you look like everyone else," said Stitch Head. He looked down at her dainty, polished shoes. "You're not wearing your kicking boots . . . you always wear your kicking boots!"

"Why would I want to kick anything?" she replied.

Stitch Head gasped in shock and horror. "What's *happened* to you? Did the doctor give you something? You can't trust him, Arabella. The tie clip . . . he's *been* to the spider's lair — or close to it. He has something to do with the spider, I just know it. And now Ivo is missing and —"

"Zere you are!" came a delighted cry. Madame Venin was gliding up the garden. "My dear Arabella, what brings you out in ze cold? You will catch your death!"

Arabella looked back at the lake, as if searching for some lost memory. "I don't know, Madame Venin," she replied.

"Well, I am 'appy zat you 'ave found each other, at least!" continued Madame Venin, clapping her hands together. "Stanley, I am sorry I did not put two and two together sooner. Young Arabella is new to us, so I was not aware yesterday zat she 'ad joined ze *famille*. Ze poor thing spent yesterday in ze infirmary, recovering from a chill . . . but ze doctor looked after her."

"The doctor . . ." muttered Stitch Head.

"Come now, let us go into ze warm and I shall make you both a cup of 'ot *chocolat*," Madame Venin added.

"Yes, Madame Venin," replied Arabella, calmly taking her hand.

"Arabella, wait!" protested Stitch Head. He grabbed Arabella by the arm, but she did not react.

"Whatever is ze matter, Stanley?" asked Madame Venin.

"It's just . . ." began Stitch Head, but he knew he could not risk trusting Madame Venin with all his secrets — not yet, at least. He bit his lip and looked back at the lake. There was a small hole broken in the ice, right in front off where Arabella had been kneeling.

"It's nothing," Stitch Head said quietly.

＊＊＊＊＊＊＊＊＊＊＊＊＊＊＊＊

Stitch Head spent the rest of the day trying to get through to Arabella, but she no longer cared to listen. In fact, she no longer seemed to care about anything. It was as if everything that made her who she was had vanished overnight. What's more, she seemed to have no recollection of the previous night's horrors and insisted on calling Stitch Head "Stanley." He had hoped it was all a trick — that she had somehow escaped the spider's lair and was now acting oddly as part of some ingenious plan. But he soon realized she really had become just like all the other children at Otherways — a blank slate.

With no sign of Ivo and Arabella lost to him, Stitch Head did what he always did in a time of crisis — he waited for night. As he watched the encroaching darkness from a dormitory window, he felt his resolve intensify. One way or another, he was going to get to the bottom of this mystery.

And he knew exactly where to start.

THE FIFTEENTH CHAPTER

LOOKING FOR ANSWERS

(Doctors and discoveries)

MAD MUSING No. 431

"Science without madness is like
a castle without monsters."

From *The Occasionally Scientific
Writings of Professor Erasmus Erasmus*

S titch Head lay in bed. He wondered if he might hear Ivo calling for help, but no call came. Perhaps he had managed to escape the spider's lair. Perhaps he was on his way back to the castle for help, and it was only a matter of time before Ivo, the Creature, Pox, and an army of creations came to the rescue. Perhaps.

In the distance he heard Madame Venin singing softly to herself. He knew he needed proof if she were to believe him — proof of a *monster* beneath Otherways.

When all was quiet, Stitch Head took a deep breath and crept out of bed. He tiptoed his way downstairs, through the hall, and down a long corridor to the doctor's study. He stretched up and tried the handle.

Locked . . . shouldn't be too hard to open, he thought. Stitch Head had become something of an expert in picking locks.

Being chased through the castle by crazy monsters on a regular basis gave him lots of practice. He slipped a thin metal lock pick from the sole of his shoe and slipped it into the lock. After a few moments there was a *CLICK!* and a *CLACK!* and the door swung open. Stitch Head checked to make sure no one was coming, then hurried inside.

The curtains were open, so bright moonlight streamed into the study. The room was large and cluttered. Shelves were crammed with folders and books, and boxes were piled on the floor. At one end of the room was a small examination table covered with a large white sheet . . . but Stitch Head's eyes were immediately drawn to the other wall. It was plastered with dozens of pictures — diagrams and studies of all kinds of spiders. Some were fat and long, with thick, hairy appendages. Others small and round, with legs as thin as thread.

Stitch Head glanced back at the examination table. There was something familiar underneath the table — his potion bag! The doctor had taken it!

He hurried over and picked it up. He was halfway through checking to see if all the bottles and potions were there safe and sound when —

"*Owww . . .*"

Stitch Head leaped back with a start. The white sheet on top of the examination table seemed to rise up of its own accord. A moment later, it fell from the table to reveal . . .

"Ivo!" cried Stitch Head. "You're all right!"

"I am not so much feeling like I am all right," Ivo replied, rubbing his eyes and straightening his bonnet. "I feel like I have been on receiving end of my own worst nightmare."

"What happened? How did you get out of the spider's lair?" asked Stitch Head. "And how did I, for that matter?"

"I remember seeing horrible, giant spider monster . . . and then wall . . . and then nothing," he began. "Then I woke up and saw strange old doctor, but he pointed stick at me and —"

"Find what you were looking for?" came a snarling voice.

Stitch Head spun around just in time to see the doctor lunge wildly at them with his cane. A jet of white gas shot out of the stick and engulfed Ivo's face. He immediately slumped back onto the table, unconscious.

"Gadsbodkins, it's so hard to get the dose right when it comes to sleeping gas," the doctor complained. "Too much and they sleep for days . . . too little and it barely lasts an hour."

"Sorry! Please, I didn't mean — um, I was just —" blurted Stitch Head.

"Balderdash! No more lies! I know exactly who you are. I've known from the start!" the doctor snarled. "At first I wasn't sure *why* you were here . . . but it is clear to me now! *He* sent you, didn't he? He sent you to take her back!"

"Sent me? No one sent me . . ." replied Stitch Head.

"Baloney! You are three feet tall with an ash-gray complexion and made up of all manner of different parts. Oh, and you have no nose," the doctor growled. "I may not be a mad professor, but I know a *creation* when I see one."

"W-what?" stuttered Stitch Head.

"Oh, come now," tutted the doctor. "You *are* a creation of *Professor Erasmus Erasmus*, are you not?"

Stitch Head's mouth dropped open.

"H-how do you know my . . . the professor?"
he asked, a chill running down his spine.

"Know him? I should say I know him!"
cried the doctor. "My name is *Doctor Edmund
Erasmus* . . . I am your master's *brother*."

THE TRAGIC TALE OF THE DOOMED LOVE OF DOCTOR EDMUND ERASMUS

(A small patch of common ground)

No time to prepare,
Don't waste it in prayer,
The spider is coming —
There's nothing to fear.

Doctor Edmund Erasmus

"You're the professor's *brother*?" Stitch Head rubbed his head, trying to make sense of the doctor's revelation.

"My name is *Doctor Edmund Erasmus*," the doctor repeated. "And *you* are my brother's first creation. I saw you the day I left Castle Grotteskew . . . the day *before* young Erasmus planned to bring you to almost-life."

"You were there when —" began Stitch Head.

"When you were put together, yes," the doctor continued. "I said he would not succeed . . . Gadsbodkins, I was wrong! Or perhaps I just didn't want him to succeed. Erasmus was always the favorite. Father didn't care for my love of spiders. It was science, but not *mad* science. When it came to deciding who would become the next mad professor of Grotteskew, I knew he would choose Erasmus. That's when I decided to leave the castle for good!

I doubt Erasmus even noticed I left. He never thought of anyone but himself."

"He left me locked in a room for forty years . . ." added Stitch Head in agreement.

"He never once wrote to me, never tried to find me," sighed the doctor. "All he ever seemed to care about . . ."

". . . was his next experiment," said Stitch Head. He and the doctor looked at each other for a moment, disturbed but strangely comforted by this small patch of common ground they shared.

"Gadsbodkins! Don't try to change the subject!" cried the doctor suddenly. "I know why you're here — you can't fool me! Well, you cannot take her! Madame Venin belongs here, with me!"

"Madame Venin?" repeated Stitch Head. "I don't understand. I'm not —"

"My brother must have spied me outside the castle and sent you to follow me — to take her back! It's not enough that he got the brains, the career, the castle — now he wants to take my precious Madame Venin from me!"

"That's not true! I came here to rescue my friend Arabella! *That's* why I followed you here, I promise!" cried Stitch Head.

The doctor adjusted his glasses and peered at Stitch Head. "Wait . . . so you're *not* here to take Madame Venin back to the professor?" he said.

"No, I swear! I don't have the slightest idea what's going on! Why would the professor want Madame Venin? He doesn't even know her . . . does he?"

The doctor sighed. Stitch Head wasn't sure whether he was relieved, or sad, or both.

"Back then, her name was not Madame Venin, but *Veronique*," he began. "We were in love . . . she was the only person who ever really cared for me. I knew I would not be truly happy until we were married! I crafted a gorgeous engagement ring from the rarest and most precious metals, then I took Veronique picnicking on the coast. It was a beautiful spot on the edge of a cliff, overlooking the sea. Everything was perfect. So I took the ring out of my pocket and popped the question. But tragedy struck — she was so surprised by my proposal that she stumbled back . . . and tumbled off the edge of the cliff!"

"Oh no . . ."

"She fell a hundred feet into icy water. But, as I hurried down the cliff face, I could see my love climbing out of the sea! She was alive! Veronique was alive! But then came the rockslide. It seems I had loosened the rocks in my climb. I leaped clear, but my love was buried beneath an avalanche of rocks and sand."

"Oh *no* . . ."

"I was sure all was lost. But a moment later, I saw Veronique struggle out of the mound of rocks. 'Gadzooks!' I cried. 'She lives!' Oh, joy of joys! Miracle of miracles! I wasted no time in placing the ring on her finger. Then she was struck by lightning."

"Oh — wait, *what*?"

"She was struck three times. Apparently the metal I had used to make her ring was some sort of *superconductor*. That was the end of her," sighed the doctor.

"Perhaps I should have accepted that our union was doomed from the start . . . but I could not bear to live without her. I could not let her go! So I did what I swore I would never do — I returned to Castle Grotteskew and begged my brother to employ his skills as a professor of mad science . . . and bring Veronique back from the grave."

"You returned to the castle?"

"My brother couldn't resist such an insane challenge. 'But be warned,' he said. 'She will not remember you, even if I bring her back.' I did not care. I just wanted to hear her voice again. I vowed that if my brother succeeded, I would dedicate each and every waking moment to giving her all that her heart desired. I waited and waited. The days turned into weeks, and I began to lose faith. Then, one night in the middle of a fearsome storm, I heard Veronique's sweet voice ring out through the castle. She was singing . . . she was alive! I rushed to the laboratory to find her, but when I got there . . ."

The doctor trailed off. He lifted his glasses and rubbed his eyes.

"When you got there, what?" asked Stitch Head.

"They say love is a kind of *madness*," he replied finally. "Perhaps I am mad! It runs in the family, after all. But I cannot forget my vow to her. I cannot!"

"What vow? I don't understand . . ."

Stitch Head saw the doctor's expression harden into a determined frown as he wheeled around to face him.

"It will all be over soon . . . there's nothing to fear," he said, pointing his cane at Stitch Head.

The sleeping gas! Stitch Head realized.

He quickly ducked as a jet of white smoke shot out from the end of the stick. Then Stitch Head raced under the doctor's legs, through the doorway, and down the corridor.

"There is no point in running, creation!" cried the doctor. "There is nothing to fear!"

"Help!" cried Stitch Head, his mind racing as fast as his legs. He looked back to see the doctor hobbling slowly after him. He was sure he could outrun him — but where should he go? There was only one choice. He followed the sound of the singing.

RETURN TO THE SPIDER'S LAIR
(Help from Madame Venin)

The spider, it abides,
You can see it in its eyes.
The rest of you are flies,
For the spider, it abides.

Doctor Edmund Erasmus

"Madame Venin! Help!" cried Stitch Head, bursting into her room. Madame Venin was at her desk, busily composing a new song.

"Stanley! What on earth is ze matter with you?" she said, leaping to her feet. "You look as if you 'ave seen *un fantôme* — a ghost!"

"Worse! It's the doctor!" Stitch Head cried. He grabbed a chair and quickly wedged it against the door behind him. "He's mad! And he's the professor's brother and he told me what happened to you and he knocked out Ivo and something's wrong with Arabella and . . . the spider! The spider is real!"

"Stanley, calm yourself, *mon petit*," said Madame Venin, placing her hand on his shoulder. "Perhaps you 'ave 'ad another nightmare?"

"No, you have to believe me! There's a

passage, hidden behind a painting — at least there *was* — if I could just find it . . ."

"Poor Stanley, you 'ave simply been fooled by ze old painting switch! Allow me to show you . . ." said Madame Venin. She glided over to a large pair of portraits on the wall. She pointed to the first. "Don't you see? When you searched for ze secret passage ze second time, you looked for ze painting you recognized — not *where* ze painting was on ze wall. All ze doctor 'ad to do was swap ze paintings around, and you would be sure to look in ze wrong place . . ."

She slipped a finger behind the second portrait and — *CLICK!* — the painting slid across the wall to reveal a passageway. It was equally as dark and cobwebbed as the other one.

"*You* have a secret passage in your room?" said Stitch Head.

"Of course! Doesn't everyone?" she

laughed. "Zis is our escape route! 'Urry! We will give ze doctor ze slip . . ."

As Madame Venin ushered Stitch Head down the dark tunnel, he decided he was either dreaming or going crazy, or possibly both.

"I don't understand! Where are we going?" he said.

"Zis way! Just a little farther," replied Madame Venin. "We are almost zere . . ."

"Almost where — AHH!"

Without warning, the floor disappeared again and Stitch Head found himself speedily sliding down a steep slope. He crashed to the floor for the second time in as many nights, landing hard on the unforgiving ground.

"Ow ow *ow* . . ." he groaned. He looked up, his head spinning and throbbing. After a brief moment, he realized the terrible truth . . .

He was back in the spider's lair.

"Watch zat last step!" chuckled Madame Venin, emerging gracefully behind him.

"What . . . ? How . . . ?" began Stitch Head as Madame Venin helped him to his feet and dusted him off. "We have to get out of here, now!"

"Oh, do *relax*, Stanley, you will give yourself an 'eadache," said Madame Venin.

"Relax?" cried Stitch Head. "This is the spider's dining room! This is where it lives. Look, that's its giant web!"

"Zat *is* a pretty big web," she admitted, inspecting the vast web that occupied one half of the chamber. "But you must trust me — zere is nothing to fear."

Stitch Head felt his borrowed blood run cold.

"What did I promise when you first arrived 'ere, *mon petit*? I promised you zat loneliness and sadness and fear would disappear," continued Madame Venin. "And it will . . . once ze spider has feasted upon your very *spirit*."

"W-what?"

"After zat, you will not worry . . . You will not care . . . You will not *feel*," continued Madame Venin. "You will do exactly as you are told without question. You will be ze ideal child — just like ze rest of zem."

"The orphans . . ." said Stitch Head.

"The spider drinks ze children's spirits like a *délicieux* milk shake!" Madame Venin cried with glee. "Each night it is *consumed* by a terrible hunger . . . and ze doctor obligingly delivers an orphan to its lair. Regular visits ensure *mes enfants* remain on ze very best behavior!"

"You knew! So you were part of it all along . . ." muttered Stitch Head, backing away in horror.

"Part of it? I am *all* of it!" said Madame Venin with a crazy laugh. "I am ze greatest creation of Mad Professor Erasmus Erasmus! I was brought back from ze darkness, one fateful night. Awakened from ze slumber of death with a new lease on almost-life . . . but I was different . . . changed . . . *better!*"

Madame Venin suddenly doubled over, and the back of her dress tore open. Stitch Head watched in horror as four long, spindly legs burst forth. Her arms and legs began to unfold over and over, doubling and tripling in length to form yet more legs. From beneath her dress, there appeared a bulbous abdomen, and from her collar burst forth a pair of massive jaws. Her eight legs tore at what remained of her dress, shredding it to ribbons as she uncurled. Within moments, the person Stitch Head knew as Madame Venin was gone. In her place stood a monstrous half-human, half-spider — a hideous, impossible mix of parts.

Madame Venin hissed, fixing both her human and spider eyes upon her prey.

"I probably should have seen this coming," squeaked Stitch Head.

THE EIGHTEENTH CHAPTER

ATTACK OF THE SPIDER
(The motion of the potion)

Shall I compare thee to a spider?
Thou art spindly legged and round,
Thou hast caught me in thy webbing,
And I am forever bound.

Doctor Edmund Erasmus

"Finally! You really 'ave no idea how uncomfortable it is keeping my spider 'alf squeezed into a dress all day! But we must keep up appearances if we are to live in ze human world, *non*?" laughed Madame Venin, stretching all eight of her long, spindly limbs. "Now zen, where was I? Oh, yes — feasting upon your *spirit*."

"AaAAH!" screamed Stitch Head as the monstrous Madame Venin attacked. He ducked under her legs again as her massive jaws swooped past his head. He dodged one leg, then another.

"Go away! My spirit tastes sour!" he cried, backing up toward the great web. "I-I'm not even totally alive!"

"You will 'ave to do!" she screamed. "I hunger!"

Stitch Head glanced at the web. It stretched all the way up to the hole in the ceiling. Plants and dry roots snaked down

from the hole. If he could climb up, he might be able to get through the hole and escape . . .

Madame Venin lunged again. He felt her spider's jaws clamp around his leg, and he kicked out with all his might. She hissed in pain and flung him into the air, sending him hurtling into the web. He grabbed one of the strands and held tight. Madame Venin reared up and fired a stream of viscous goo, binding him to the web.

"Wait! I can make a potion for you — a potion to cure you! You'll never have to drink another spirit again!" cried Stitch Head. He tried desperately to free himself as Madame Venin began to climb. She quickly circled him, her human head wide-eyed and grinning. Then she brought her huge, spirit-draining spider-fangs up to his face . . .

"Get away from him, please, crazy weird spider monster!"

Stitch Head looked up to see a tiny, oval head poking down through the hole in the ceiling. "Ivo!"

"Stitch Head! I have come here to make daring rescue!" cried Ivo.

Stitch Head saw a tiny bottle drop down from the hole and smash onto Madame

Venin's abdomen, shattering into a spray of glass and blue liquid. "Eat potion, weird creature from worst nightmare!" Ivo cried. He threw another bottle. Then another. And another!

Madame Venin screamed in rage as bottles rained down on her. She fired a strand of webbing, grabbing one bottle in midair and flinging it away. But more kept coming. Bottles of every shape and color, each filled with unpredictable and unstable potions. Madame Venin flailed and screamed as the potions exploded and mixed together, causing plumes of colored smoke to fill the air. Finally, she lost her grip on the web and tumbled to the ground.

Ivo quickly emptied the rest of the potion bag through the hole. A moment later, Madame Venin let out a blood-curdling scream as she disappeared beneath a cloud of churning, multicolored smoke.

"Turns out nature is smart, but mad science is miracles!" said Ivo.

"Ivo, you're okay!" cried Stitch Head.

"I think I am building up immunity to sleeping gas!" replied Ivo. "I awoke

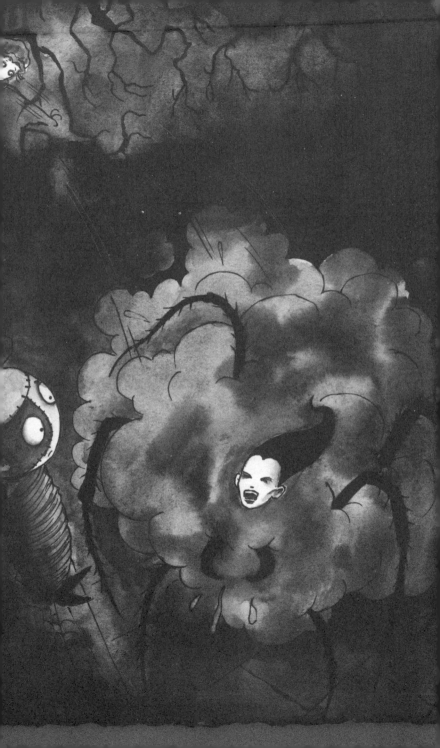

in doctor's study, so I followed terrified screams and here you are. And how was your day?"

"I'm stuck!" shouted Stitch Head. "Can you give me a hand?"

"That had better not be joke about me having one arm," warned Ivo. He leaped onto the web and climbed down to Stitch Head. "So, it turns out your favorite lady is creepy spider monster . . ."

"I noticed!" replied Stitch Head. "I think, in a way, the professor tried to make up for being their father's favorite by combining the two things that his brother loved most: Veronique and spiders. Seems about the right level of insanity for my master . . ."

Ivo busily wrenched at the webbing holding Stitch Head with his metal arm. "So," he continued, "you think potions cure her of spirit-sucking?"

As if on cue, Madame Venin leaped out of the smoke with an angry, stomach-churning cry. She landed on the web and immediately started to climb.

"Apparently not! Hang on!" cried Stitch Head, grabbing Ivo and flinging him onto his back.

Madame Venin launched a barrage of web strands as Stitch Head leaped into the air. He reached for the tree roots and scrambled up into the hole in the ceiling

and into a narrow, stone cylinder. He began to climb frantically. He looked down to see Madame Venin slamming into the small hole.

"Is horrible spider monster behind us?" asked Ivo. "None of this is doing anything to help phobia . . ."

"I don't think she can fit through!" said Stitch Head.

Soon they emerged into the cold night air. Snow was falling heavily in large, wet chunks. It took Stitch Head a moment to realize that they had climbed out of the old well in the garden. Behind them was the house . . . ahead of them, the frozen lake and dark wood. "Come on, we have to get Arabella! We have to go back to the orphanage."

"I do not think so," replied Ivo, hopping off Stitch Head's back. "Bad things happen in orphanage. In last two days, I have been dragged around by you, hit in head by giant spider, and gassed by evil doctor. I do not want to go back to orphanage!"

"I'm sorry, Ivo," began Stitch Head, "but you know we can't leave without —"

"Also, Angry Girl is over there, by lake," added Ivo. He pointed his single arm toward the frozen lake. There, kneeling by the bank in her nightdress, covered in snow, was Arabella.

FINDING ARABELLA

(On reflection)

MAD MUSING No. 774

"If at first you don't succeed,
add another leg."

From *The Occasionally Scientific
Writings of Professor Erasmus Erasmus*

"What she doing there? And why she dressed like orphan?" asked Ivo.

"That's where I found her this morning," Stitch Head replied. They raced over to her. "Arabella! Get up! We have to go!"

"I d-don't want to go," she said, shivering in the cold. "Otherways is m-m-my home."

"No, that's not true! This isn't you — you're not yourself!" said Stitch Head. He tried to lift Arabella. But she shrugged him off and knelt back down, still staring at the lake. "Arabella, Madame Venin took your spirit — she made you forget who you are. Please, you have to come with us!"

"Or at least go indoors — I cannot feel toes," added Ivo. Arabella continued to stare absently at the lake. "What is Angry Girl looking at, anyway?"

Stitch Head leaned over Arabella's shoulder. He peered into the pool of water and saw his own face staring back at him.

"She made a hole in the ice," he said. "I think she wanted to see her reflection."

"It d-doesn't look like me," stuttered Arabella, pointing at her reflection.

"That's right! It's not you, Arabella!" replied Stitch Head. "Don't let them take away who you are! You're Arabella — strong, noisy, loyal . . ."

"Kicky . . ." Ivo added.

"And you're our friend!" cried Stitch Head. He took his potion bag from Ivo and pulled out the only thing left inside it: Arabella's doll. He put it into her hands and wrapped her fingers around it. "We came to bring you back because we're your friends. We're your *family*."

"Grandma . . ." she said, gripping the doll.

"Sorry, it look better with clothes on," said Ivo, dusting the snow off his dress. Arabella gazed up at Stitch Head. He saw a tear roll down her cheek.

"I want to g-go home," she whispered. "To the castle."

"Now *that* sounds like a plan," replied Stitch Head, helping her up. "Let's get out of here before —"

KRooOOooM!

The well shattered into pieces. Great chunks of stone flew across the garden in all directions. A moment later, Madame Venin burst forth. She clambered out into the cold snow with a savage hiss and set her

sights on Stitch Head and Ivo, who stood frozen in shock.

"And where do you think you're going?" she cried. "I hunger!"

"Now we run away again?" said Ivo.

"Now we run away again!" replied Stitch Head. "Go!"

ESCAPE ACROSS THE ICE
(Family ties)

Oh, my love is like a spider's web,
All glittering and strong.
I could stare at you for hours,
Never tiring of your song.

Doctor Edmund Erasmus

"There is nowhere to go! We are stuck between spider monster and lake!" cried Ivo. Madame Venin scuttled angrily through the snow toward them.

"Come on! This way!" Stitch Head shouted, pulling Ivo and Arabella across the frozen lake. They skidded and slipped on the slick surface. The thin ice strained and cracked beneath their feet. Stitch Head looked back to see Madame Venin scuttling through the snow after them. She roared in rage, stopping at the bank and testing the ice with a spindly leg.

"Crazy spider monster does not like to ice skate!" said Ivo happily. "We are safe now!"

"Come back! I hunger!" wailed Madame Venin. She scurried left and right, back and forth, wondering whether she could go around the lake and reach her prey before it vanished into the woods.

With a hungry howl, she stepped onto the ice, first with four legs . . . then all eight. She slid across it, her legs flailing in all directions as it cracked and splintered.

Stitch Head looked to the woods and then back at Madame Venin. She had steadied herself and was already darting across the lake toward them at top speed, but Stitch Head was sure they would make it unless —

"YooOWAah!"

Stitch Head's feet slid out from under him, and he tumbled onto the ice, taking Arabella and Ivo down with him. The ice fractured and splintered in all directions, and Stitch Head felt cold water seep up from underneath.

"Don't move a muscle!" he cried. "If the ice gives way . . ."

"I hunger!" screamed Madame Venin. She was closing in!

"Gadsbodkins! Stop!" came a cry. Stitch Head glanced toward the bank. The doctor was on the frozen lake, limping and skidding awkwardly toward Madame Venin. "Stop!

Veronique, my love! Come back! The ice is too thin!"

Madame Venin hissed in rage as the doctor jabbed his cane into the ice to steady himself. The cane was sending great cracks splintering across the lake.

"Doctor, you fool, turn back!" growled Madame Venin.

"I will not lose you, my love! Not again!" the doctor cried, still slowly hobbling toward her. "I vowed that day I would give you everything you desired — even though you had been turned into a monstrous half-human, half-spider cursed with an insatiable appetite for human spirits! I looked after you, I created a disguise for you . . . I built the orphanage and brought you children to feed upon!"

"*Oui, oui* — I can't *keep* saying thank you." Madame Venin said with a sigh.

"I gave up everything for you!" cried

the doctor. "But I won't let you throw your almost-life away for the sake of your hunger! Now please, give me your leg! I will pull you to shore!"

"Get back! Ze ice is too thin for us both!" Madame Venin cried again. The doctor continued edging toward her. "Back, I say!"

Sharp cracks of fragmenting ice echoed through the air, and freezing water glugged up onto the surface of the lake. Madame Venin looked back at Stitch Head as he finally managed to get everyone on their feet.

"I hunger!" she hissed again.

"Please, my love! Come with me!" said the doctor, throwing his arms around Madame Venin. "I couldn't bear to be without my lovely Veronique! Gadsbodkins, we belong together!"

Madame Venin had time to cry "Get

back!" one more time before the ice gave way. The center of the lake splintered in a perfect circle, shattering into a thousand shards. Madame Venin and the doctor plunged into the black, icy water. Within moments, they were gone.

A HUNDRED ORPHANS
(The new plan)

MAD MUSING No. 95

"There is strength in numbers.
Of tentacles."

From *The Occasionally Scientific
Writings of Professor Erasmus Erasmus*

"They're . . . they're gone," muttered Stitch Head as the bubbling ripples began to fade. They were inches from the edge of the dark water where the ice had given way.

"There was nothing you could do," said Ivo, taking Stitch Head's arm and patting it gently. "But we will be gone also, unless we get off ice."

"He's right — I ain't waiting here," said Arabella as the ice continued to crack beneath their feet. The three of them inched gingerly to the shore and scrambled onto the soft snow.

"I am not leaving castle anymore," said Ivo. "Monsters in big, wide world are *much* worse than monsters in castle."

"Arabella . . . are you okay?" asked Stitch Head. Arabella brushed the snow out of her hair, ruffling it into a familiar tangled mess.

"Yeah, I'm back," she said. "Ain't quite feeling myself yet, but nothing a few kicks won't cure."

She looked again at her doll, and then turned to Ivo. "Reckon you should keep the dress," Arabella said. "Looks better on you, anyway."

"Thank you," said Ivo, "I am starting to like it."

Stitch Head, Arabella, and Ivo made their way back to the orphanage with a single goal in mind — getting home to Castle Grotteskew. There was just one problem. What to do with the orphans?

"Do we just leave 'em all here?" said Arabella. They stood in the dormitory, watching the children sleep. "I mean, where else are they going to go?"

"But soon their spirits will return, like yours," added Ivo. "Then they will care about all the things they have not cared about. They will say, 'Who will look after us?' and 'Where we go?' and 'Why we all dressed in same silly clothes?'"

"Says the creation in a frilly dress," said Arabella.

"Maybe the humans know what to do," continued Ivo. "Maybe we say to humans of Grubbers Nubbin, 'Hello, we have found one hundred orphans. Would you like to give them home and be their new family?'"

"There's too many of them," said Arabella. "They'll just end up in another orphanage."

"*Humans and creations . . .*" muttered Stitch Head finally.

"You okay, Stitch Head?" asked Arabella. Stitch Head rubbed his eyes and shook his head.

"Yesterday, Madame Venin gave me a coin to throw into the well — into the spider's lair," he said. "She told me to make a wish."

"Did you wish she was weird spider monster?" asked Ivo.

"I wished we were all back in the castle, safe and sound in our home . . . I wished for all the things the orphans don't have." Stitch Head took a deep, long breath. "We need to wake up the orphans. We're taking them with us . . . We're taking them back to Castle Grotteskew."

THE TWENTY-SECOND CHAPTER

THE JOURNEY HOME
(Creations, meet humans)

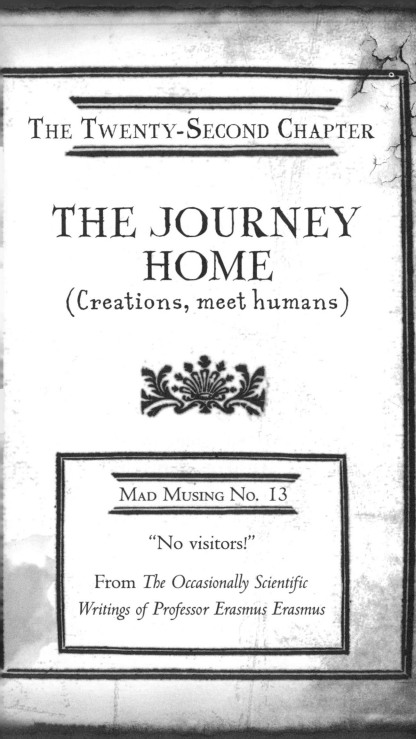

MAD MUSING No. 13

"No visitors!"

From *The Occasionally Scientific
Writings of Professor Erasmus Erasmus*

Stitch Head, Arabella, Ivo, and one hundred orphans made their way through the snow in the middle of the night. The journey was long and bitterly cold, but the orphans did not complain. They walked in silence, putting one foot in front of the other like a band marching to a drum.

"Do you really think children will like castle full of monsters?" asked Ivo as they trudged along a moonlit road. "I am thinking there will be a lot of terrified screaming."

"Yeah, they ain't going to be like this when they get their spirits back," said Arabella. "They're going to be like real kids, running and shouting and kicking."

"I know," nodded Stitch Head. He paused for a moment. "Um — are they all going to be like you?"

"Nah, don't worry," said Arabella, giving

Stitch Head a friendly punch on the arm.
"I'm one of a kind."

As dawn began to break over the distant
hills, Stitch Head spotted a welcome and
familiar sight — the bleak, shadowy form
of Castle Grotteskew. They made their way
past Grubbers Nubbin with their army of
strange orphan children, toward the steep
hill.

The sun had almost risen by the time
they began the climb to the castle. To
Stitch Head, it was the longest part of the
journey. He had never felt so homesick in
his almost-life. As they trudged up the hill,
he heard a cry on the wind. He peered up
at the castle parapet to see the Creature,
waving something and shouting, "They're
BACK! They're BACK!" at the top of its
lungs.

"What's the Creature got there? Is that a *banner*?" asked Arabella.

"It's very heartfelt," Stitch Head replied with a grin.

As they reached the Great Door, it swung open. The Creature stamped out, bawling with happiness and relief. It abandoned its banner to lift Arabella into a three-armed embrace.

"ARABELLA!" it boomed. "Stitch Head, you DID it!"

"Hey, get off me, you big dope — I told you I don't do hugs," complained Arabella. Pox flew down with a "SWaaaRTiKi!" and started gleefully chewing on her hair.

Stitch Head smiled and began leading the orphans inside. They gathered obediently in the courtyard and stood there in silence. After a moment, the creations of Castle Grotteskew began to appear from the darkness, nervously edging out into the light. They muttered to each other suspiciously, not daring to get too close to their new guests.

"What in the name of my third eye is going on?"

"Humans and creations? It can't be done!"

"They seem well behaved, at least . . ."

"THIS is going to be GREAT!"

"I think this may be calm before storm," whispered Ivo.

Stitch Head shook his head, not quite able to believe what had happened. He had ventured out beyond the castle to bring back one orphan, not one hundred and one!

"Creations in the real world, humans in Castle Grotteskew . . . everything's changed," he said. "And maybe it's about time."

About the Author

Guy Bass is an award-winning writer, author, and stuff. In 2010 he won the Blue Peter Book Award for Most Fun Book With Pictures for *Dinkin Dings and the Frightening Things* and has twice won the Portsmouth Book Award (Shorter Novel) for his Dinkin Dings series. Guy grew up dreaming of being a superhero — he even had a Spider-Man costume. The costume doesn't fit anymore, so Guy now contents himself with writing children's books and drawing the occasional picture. Guy lives in London with his wife and no dog, yet.

About the Illustrator

Pete Williamson lives in a garden flat in South London with his girlfriend. He has worked as a designer for an animation company and also as a psychiatric nurse. Pete's interests include peculiar music, good books, and drinking too much coffee.

WANT MORE CREEPY CREATIONS AND MAD PROFESSORS?

CHECK OUT THESE OTHER BOOKS IN THE STITCH HEAD SERIES!

Something BIG is about to happen to someone SMALL.

Join a mad professor's forgotten creation as he steps out of the shadows and into the adventure of an almost-lifetime.

Someone SMALL
is about to set sail
on a BIG adventure.

Join a mad professor's
forgotten creation
as he prepares for
an almost-life on
the high seas.

Someone SMALL
is about to discover
a BIG secret.

Join a mad professor's
forgotten creation
as he fights for his
very heart and soul.

First published in the United States in 2015
by Capstone Young Readers
A Capstone Imprint
1710 Roe Crest Drive
North Mankato, Minnesota 56003
www.capstoneyoungreaders.com

First published by
Stripes Publishing Ltd.
1 The Coda Centre, 189 Munster Road
London SW6 6AW

Cataloging-in-Publication Data is available
on the Library of Congress website.

ISBN: 978-1-62370-192-5

Summary:
When Arabella ends up an orphanage, Stitch Head leaves
Grotteskew and all its creatures behind in a daring rescue attempt.
Stitch Head is confident he can save his cranky friend — until he
crosses paths with a gruesome monster and gets trapped in a web
he can't escape . . .

Printed in China by Nordica
0515/CA21500779
052015   008956R

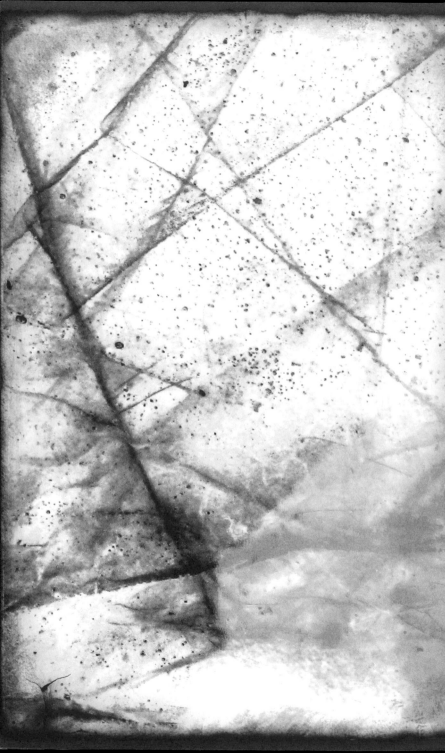